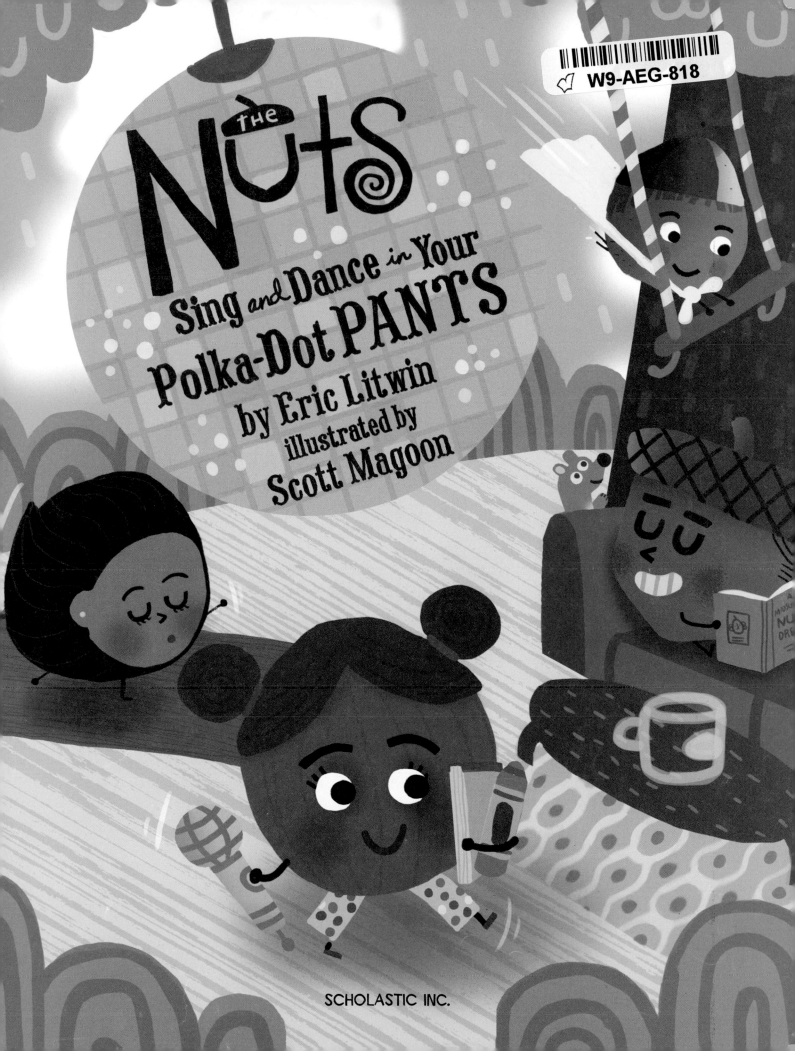

The Nuts
Sing and Dance in Your Polka-Dot PANTS

by Eric Litwin

illustrated by Scott Magoon

SCHOLASTIC INC.

Hazel loved to sing and dance.
Hazel loved her polka-dot pants.

Polka-dot pants.

Polka-dot pants.

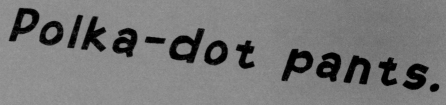

Sing and dance
in your
polka-dot pants.

Oh, No!

Papa's nose
was stuck in a book.
He didn't see Hazel.
He didn't even look.

WOULD PAPA DANCE?
NOT A CHANCE.

But Hazel kept rocking
in her polka-dot pants.

Polka-dot pants.

Polka-dot pants.

Sing and dance
in your
polka-dot pants.

Oh, No!

Mama Nut
was crazy busy.
She ran up and down
in a dizzy tizzy.

WOULD MAMA SING?
NOT A CHANCE.
WOULD PAPA DANCE?
NOT A CHANCE.

But Hazel kept rocking
in her polka-dot pants.

Oh, No!

Her little brother,
Wally Nut,
was being a pain
in the you-know-what.

WOULD WALLY PLAY?
NOT A CHANCE.
WOULD MAMA SING?
NOT A CHANCE.
WOULD PAPA DANCE?
NOT A CHANCE.

But Hazel kept rocking
in her polka-dot pants.

Oh, No!

Hazel Nut rocked all alone.
So Hazel Nut picked up the phone.
Hazel knew just what to say.

WHO DID HAZEL CALL THAT DAY?

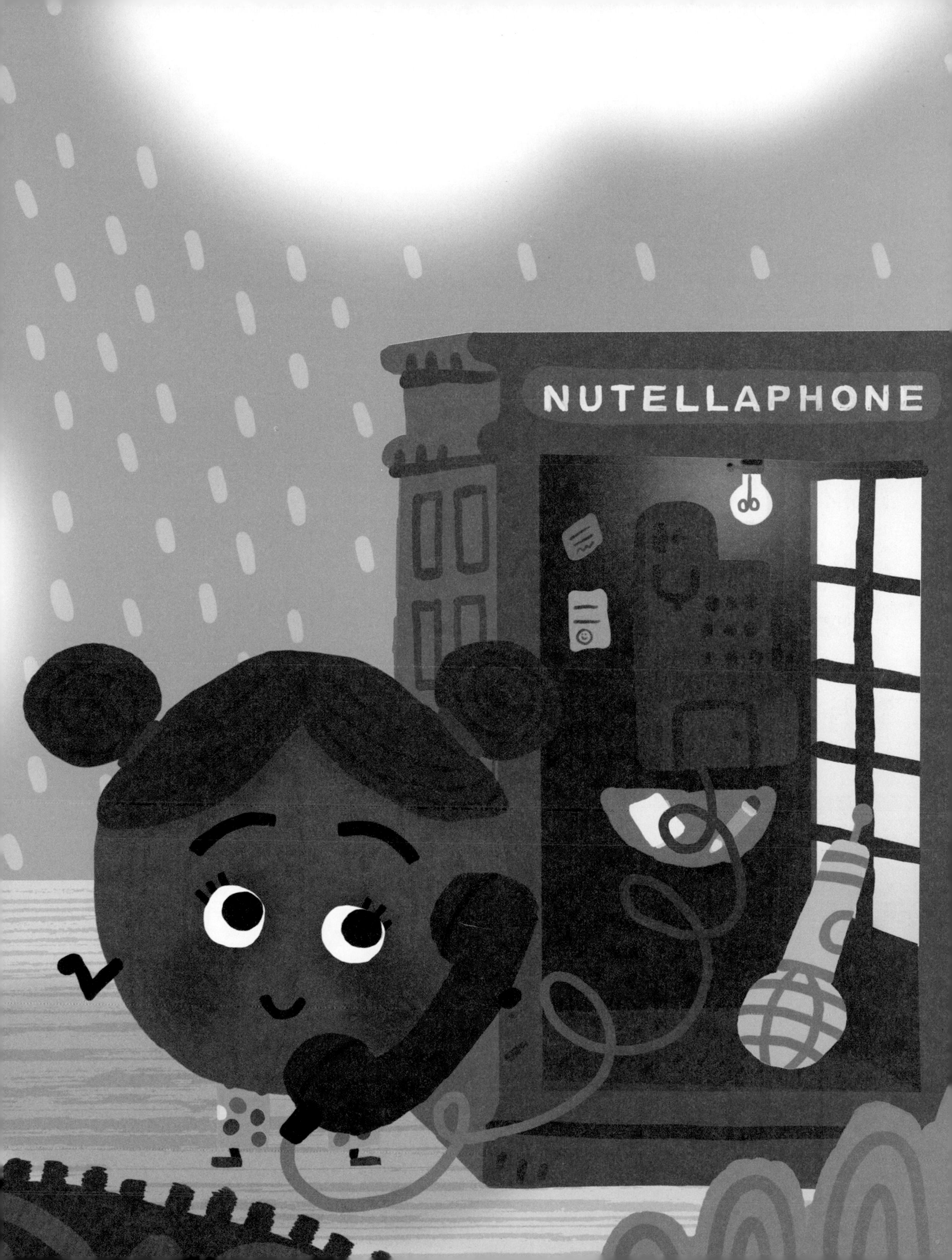
NUTELLAPHONE

GRANDMA NUT
burst through the door.
She disco-danced
across the floor.
She said, "Grandma loves you
through and through,

so Grandma Nut's going to
ROCK WITH YOU."

Polka-dot pants.

Polka-dot pants.

Sing and dance
in your polka-dot pants.

Oh, Yes!

Mama, Papa, and Wally, too, heard that happy hullabaloo.

The next thing they knew
they were tapping their feet.

Their heads began bopping
to the bop-able beat.

They started to sing.
They got up to dance.
And that family rocked together
in their polka-dot pants.

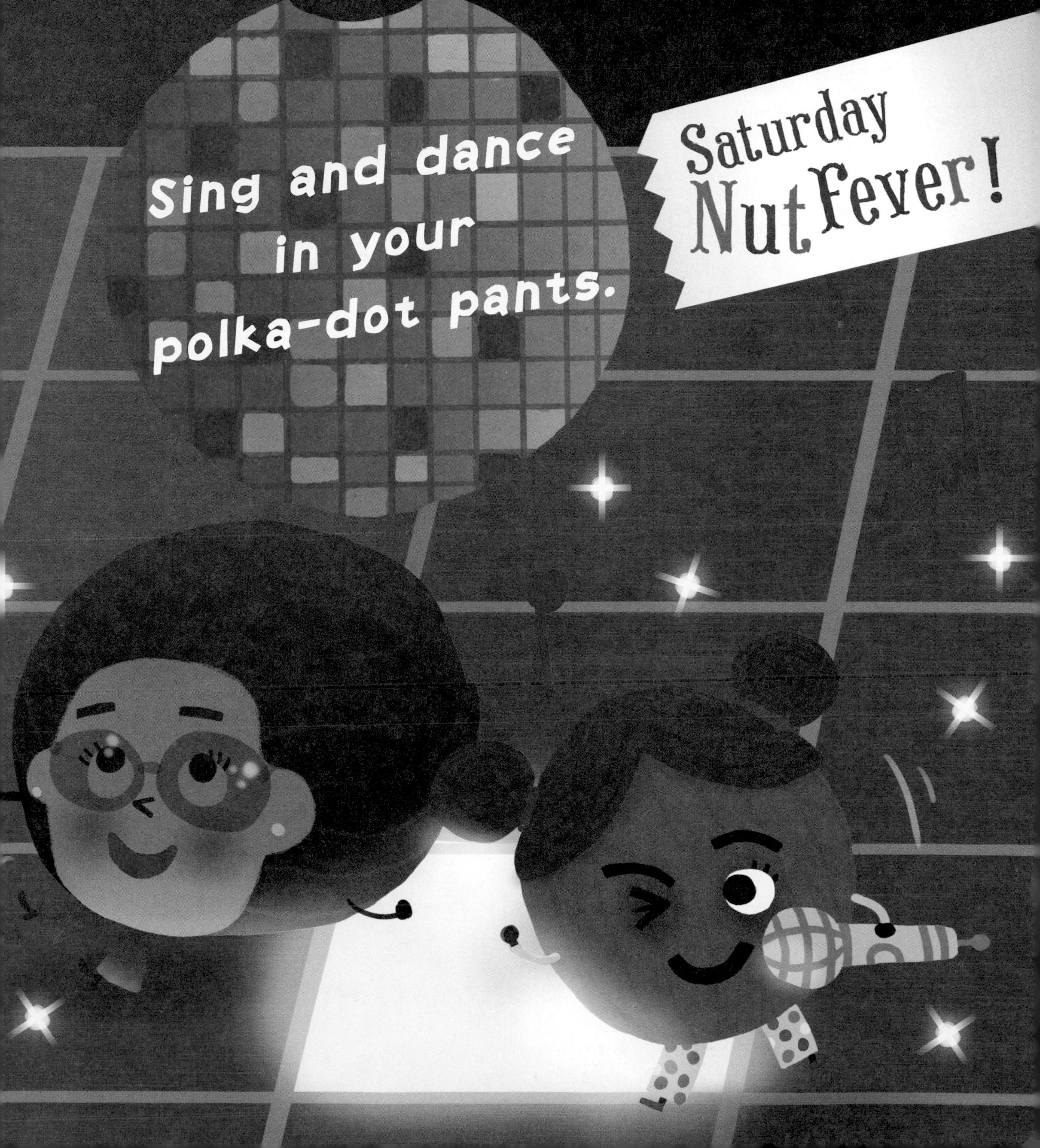

DO THE POLKA-DOT PANTS DANCE!

Polka-dot do-do-do.

Polka-dot pants,
polka-dot pants.

Polka-dot do-do-do.

Polka-dot
pants dance!

Go up,  go down,

go up, go round
and round.

Go this way, go that way,

go this way, go every way!

To the front, to the back,

to the front,

and then clap clap clap!

Download free songs and dance along at TheNutFamily.com!

To the Fantastically Fun Fishman Family —EL

For everyone out on this dance floor—keep bustin'! —SM

About This Book

This book was edited by Allison Moore and Liza Baker and designed by Krisuna Iulo with art direction by Saho Fujii.
The digital illustrations were created using Adobe Photoshop and a very nutty imagination.
The text and display type were set in Skizzors, and the cover was hand-lettered by the illustrator.

ISBN 978-1-338-10649-7

12 11 10 9 8 7 6 5 4 3 2 1   16 17 18 19 20 21

Printed in the U.S.A.   40

First Scholastic printing, September 2018